The Lost Filly

A Horse-Crazy Adventure

Written and Illustrated by

Jean Russell Nave

May horse love always be in your life.

[signature]

Windemere Press

Sisters, Oregon 97759

The Lost Filly

Copyright 2014

Windemere Press, Sisters, Oregon 97759

Juvenile Fiction/Middle Grade – Ages 9 and up

Printed in the

United States of America.

ISBN-13: 978-1495403255
ISBN-10: 1495403254

Other recent books by Jean (Russell) Nave

The Harry and Lola Collection

The Harry and Lola Christmas Collection

Harry and Lola Meet the Dragon

Harry and Lola Meet MacDuffer

Harry and Lola Meet Starprancer (The book that started the Horse Crazy Series)

Contents

1

Illness

*An explosion rocked the ship. Fire licked the heels of a big black horse as he dove into the dark, roiling sea. A young girl followed the horse into the swirling waters, falling...falling...*jolting Josie awake. Groggily, she opened her eyes and looked out the window of the moving car.

The rain had finally stopped. The windshield wipers were no longer thumping, so at last there was relief for her throbbing head.

She and her aunt had been driving through rain for nearly half the night.

Between her fitful naps and the thump, thump, thumping of the windshield wipers, Josie had developed a nasty headache.

She opened her big brown eyes just as the SUV reached the summit of Santiam Pass. They were heading east into Central Oregon. The clear, early morning sky greeting her was dark purple. A hint of lavender marked the eastern horizon, ahead of the rising sun.

As Josie watched, the sky turned a brilliant pink. Then, suddenly, the golden edge of the sun flickered at the top of the Ochoco Mountains, far to the east.

Looking to her right, she saw the dramatic eastern slopes of the Cascade Mountains as they reflected the sunrise. The snowcapped peaks looked like pink marshmallows. Slowly, giant golden sunrays reached across the sky painting the heights with shimmering yellows and pinks. Finally, as the car descended the eastern side of the pass, the rising sun changed the mountains into white marble peaks.

"Wow" said Josie, to Aunt Sue, who was driving the car. "I've never seen a sunrise like that before."

"Welcome to Central Oregon," said Aunt Sue. "Josie, it may not be easy for you to live with us, but I think you'll see this is really beautiful country. I hope you'll be able to find some happiness as all the pain passes."

The pain will never pass, thought Josie, as she remembered the night she had just gone through.

*****

She had come home from the last day of school, thinking that maybe this would be a different summer vacation.

Josie was finally twelve. She would be thirteen when school started in the fall—old enough to take care of herself. She would not need Mrs. Williams looking after her during the long summer days while her mom worked.

Josie was small for her age, but her dark brown hair and piercing brown eyes made her look more mature, in spite of her height. Most people thought she was a teenager, though she didn't quite look old enough to drive.

Josie hoped that maybe this summer she could have some fun. Maybe she could finally hang out with her friends at the park or the mall. Maybe she would even get to go to some movies. She would have to find a way to earn a little money—money that would be hers, that she could spend any way she wanted.

Josie lived with her mom, Carol. It had been so long since she had seen her father that she didn't even remember what he looked like. Her mom and dad had divorced when Josie was six years old while they were living in Southern California.

Two years ago her mom announced that they were moving to Portland, Oregon. Carol had a sister living in Oregon and she was filled with hope that life could be better in the clean, moist air of the Pacific Northwest.

Though Portland was bustling, Carol had not been able to find a job paying much more than minimum wage. They'd ended up living in a dilapidated apartment in a rundown, eastside neighborhood.

****

Earlier, as Josie had opened the door to their apartment, thinking about summer vacation, she'd heard moaning coming from the apartment's one bedroom.

Snapped from her thoughts, she ran into the room and looked at her mom lying in the bed. Carol's red face was covered with sweat; her gray streaked hair was matted, clinging to her clammy skin.

"Mom!" cried Josie. "What's wrong?"

"Thank goodness you're finally home," rasped Carol. "I don't know what's wrong but I'm really sick. Call Aunt Sue and ask her to come."

Josie ran to the telephone, looked up Aunt Sue's number and dialed it.

"Hello?" answered the woman's voice at the other end of the call.

"Aunt Sue!" yelled Josie into the telephone. "Mom's really sick. I'm scared. She needs your help right now. Please come! If you saw her, you'd be scared too!"

Josie started to cry.

"Calm down, Josie," said Aunt Sue. "You know your mom sometimes overreacts. She's never as sick as she thinks."

"She is this time!" cried Josie. "Please come. I know it's a long way to drive, but I'm really scared. She's your sister. You should care enough to help her."

Ever since Carol and Josie had moved to Oregon, things had not gone well between the two sisters. Carol's lack of success with work and the poor conditions in which they lived had been a constant source of irritation.

There were other issues that Josie didn't understand. Maybe she never would. All she knew right now was that her mother *was* really, really sick. Someone had to help her take care of her mom.

"What time is it?" asked Aunt Sue as she looked at her watch, "Oh, I see. It's a little after four. You know it's a three hour drive to get there don't you?"

There was a long pause on the phone and then Aunt Sue continued, "I've got to put dinner together for Sam, pack a few things for staying overnight and then I'll leave. I'll see you at about eight. OK?"

"Thank you, Aunt Sue," said Josie.

Josie stood there for a minute looking at the telephone, tears streaming down her face. After catching her breath and drying her tears, she walked back into her mom's bedroom.

"She's coming," said Josie. "What else do you want me to do?"

Her mom just shook her head and closed her fever-red eyes.

2

The Orphan

That night Josie fixed dinner for herself: toast and a can of tomato soup. She offered some soup to her mom, but Carol didn't want anything but a glass of water.

Then Josie sat down to watch television. She didn't own any video games. Carol had said she didn't like the violence. Josie knew the real reason was that they couldn't afford them. But she had her favorite movie on DVD, *The Black Stallion*.

Josie had gotten the movie last Christmas. She'd probably watched it a hundred times and knew most of the dialogue by heart. She never got tired of watching that beautiful black horse run through the turquoise surf of the desert island. And when Alec Ramsey raced the Black Stallion in New York she could feel the wind streaking tears across her face. It was as if she were riding the big horse as it raced around the oval track, beating the two champion racehorses of the time.

Turning on the DVD player, Josie wanted to get lost in the sounds and pictures. She needed to float away from the pain and fear shrouding the apartment.

Instead, even while watching her favorite movie, time dragged as Josie watched the clock and waited for Aunt Sue to arrive.

Periodically she looked in on her mother. Carol sometimes slept, sometimes thrashed in the bed, and often moaned. But she wouldn't let Josie call 911 nor did she want any other help. She just wanted her sister.

At half past eight Aunt Sue knocked on the door. Josie let in the trim, spry woman, noticing that her gray eyes showed she was not happy about coming. But as soon as Aunt Sue saw Carol, her attitude changed. Aunt Sue realized that her younger sister really was sick.

"Let me call 911," Aunt Sue demanded. But Carol refused. Then Aunt Sue closed the door, leaving Josie outside to wonder what was going on.

She heard the women talking. Carol moaned a few times. Then, Aunt Sue screamed and ran out the door grabbing Josie, hugging her close.

"Oh, Josie!" cried Aunt Sue. "She's gone! Just like that and she's gone! We've got to call 911."

The rest of the night was a blur. Emergency people came and left. Neighbors and friends stopped by, talked to Aunt Sue, and told Josie they were so sorry.

Aunt Sue made important arrangements to take care of things related to Carol's death. Then she packed a box with Josie's few personal possessions and put it in the car.

"We're going home, Josie," said Aunt Sue.

"But this is my home!" cried Josie.

"Not anymore," said Aunt Sue. "You'll come live with me and Sam at least until things get settled. You can stay in Jack's old room."

****

So they had driven in the rain for hours until reaching the crest of the Cascade Mountains, where the rain finally stopped and the sun lit up the morning sky.

Josie had slept fitfully during the drive. She had dreamed that she was the one, not Alec Ramsey, who was cast into the raging sea. In her dream the big black horse did save her and pull her to the desert island. But she never got to ride the horse. She never even came close to it. In her dream the horse always ran away and screamed a shrill, piercing cry, as if he was terrified of life. The horse in her dream was as scared as Josie felt right now.

****

Josie had only visited Aunt Sue's home once in the two years she and her mom had lived in Oregon.

"It costs too much to drive out there," her mother had said. But now Josie was going to be living in this high desert country. What did the future hold for a twelve year old orphan?

At last Aunt Sue pulled onto the gravel driveway leading to the house. The first thing Josie saw was the empty corral.

Jack, Aunt Sue's son, had once owned a horse. The corral and barn had now been empty for years. Josie noticed how the native bunch grass grew, filling in between the rocks. The corral fence, made of sturdy posts, cross rails and wire fencing, looked like it was in good condition.

A momentary thrill ran through Josie. If she lived here, could she get a horse and put it in the corral?

Josie quickly banished the thought. Horses cost a lot of money, and now she was an orphan. How could she ever afford a horse?

As they passed the barn she saw the house. It was a real house, not a duplex or an apartment, but a house. It wasn't fancy, but it was a clean and fresh two-story house. And Aunt Sue had said she could stay in Jack's room. She'd have her own room.

Josie remembered how, during that one visit she and her mom had made when they first moved to Oregon, she had peeked into Jack's room.   There had been horse posters and photographs on the walls, lots of them. Were they still there?

Jack had already moved out at the time of her visit. He'd joined the Marines and was off fighting a war in some far away country. But his room had been neat and clean, as if he would be coming home at any time.

If the photos and posters were still on the walls, Josie thought she could be comfortable staying in his room. Lots of pictures of horses would help warm her aching heart.

Then she thought about her mom. She was never going to see her mom again. Never going to be able to laugh with her or share her dreams with her again.

Josie's mom had loved horses too. She'd always told Josie that "someday" they would have the money to buy a house and have a horse. She'd said Josie would be able to ride her horse all summer long…someday.

Now Josie knew that dream had died with her mom.

****

"OK," said Aunt Sue. "Let's get something to eat. I'm sure you're hungry. Then we can sleep for a while.

"We can talk about the future once we've had some food and rest. Take your things upstairs to Jack's room and I'll fix us some scrambled eggs."

Josie remembered that Jack's room was on the left overlooking the corral. Easing herself through the door, she looked around. The horse photos and posters were still there. Most of them were photos of Jack on his big bay. He'd ridden it many years in the Sisters Rodeo Parade and had ribbons hanging next to some of the photos. *What a lucky guy*, thought Josie.

Josie quickly emptied her box. She put her clothes into an empty dresser drawer. She set out her brush and comb on the top of the dresser and started looking around the room.

It was well-appointed with square, modern oak furniture, masculine, with no frills. Everything matched—the dresser, desk, nightstands and double bed. The bedspread was a bright, Southwest Native American print. At first glance, the room looked like Jack still lived in it. But upon closer inspection, Josie realized all the drawers were empty and small personal items were gone.

Josie took special note of the X-Box game console attached to the flat screen television in the corner.

"Eggs are ready," called Aunt Sue.

Josie ran down the stairs, suddenly realizing that she was starved.

"Is there anything special you'd like for dinner?" asked Aunt Sue while they ate.

Josie shook her head. She didn't know what was in the cupboard, how could she know what could be for dinner?

The eggs, toast and fresh fruit were delicious. It was like a Sunday feast. She was so full from the wonderful breakfast that she suddenly felt sleepy. Her lack of sleep from the long night and the drive over the mountains now weighed on her. She wanted to curl up and sleep like a kitten.

Before going to her room, though, Josie helped Aunt Sue clear the dishes. They had a dishwasher, so it was really easy. All Josie had to do was rinse off the plates and put them in the dishwasher.

Once the kitchen was clean, Josie and Aunt Sue headed for their bedrooms.

Josie was asleep as soon as her head hit the pillow.

3

The Filly

When Josie woke up, the clock showed it was two o'clock in the afternoon. She had slept for four hours. Looking around Josie realized that this bedroom had its own attached bathroom.

Splashing water on her face, Josie glanced about. The bathroom was *so* big and it was hers to use! There was a marble sink, large bathtub and separate shower. Josie knew she'd miss her mom forever, but she would enjoy living with all this luxury.

Josie walked down the hall and peeked into Aunt Sue's room. She was sound asleep, so Josie decided she'd check out things around the yard.

The house was perched on the rim of a deep basalt canyon. A creek ran through tall pines and willows far below.

Josie thought she remembered how to find the trail. It hugged the canyon wall and wandered all the way down to the creek.

After a couple false starts she found the entrance to the trail. It was steep and rough. The descent to the canyon floor looked like it was about two hundred feet. Josie noticed lots of loose rocks and broken branches. It seemed like the trail wasn't used much anymore.

Josie had to climb over a few large rocks that had rolled down the cliff, partially blocking the trail. She reached the creek without tripping or falling down the steep cliff.

Turning around she looked back up the rocky canyon wall. All she could see was a small corner of the house. No one would know she was down there once she crossed the creek.

But how would she cross it? The creek was so full of fresh snowmelt that it was really more like a small river.

Josie headed down stream to see if fallen logs or large rocks would allow her to cross without having to wade through the rushing water.

She eventually came to a place where the stream spread out. The willows that had been hugging the far side of the creek opened up so that sand and pebbles shone through the shallow flow. If she took off her shoes she could wade across to the other side without fear of being swept downstream.

The creek water was cold, almost as cold as the snow it came from. Even in this site, where the stream flow widened out, the water came above her ankles. Her feet were bright pink and she was shivering from the cold by the time she reached the far side.

After crossing, Josie sat on a large rock to warm her feet and put on her shoes.

The air was pleasantly warm. Josie smelled the sweet, spicy fragrance of the aspen trees. The high country, water loving tree's roots spread out like spider webs in the mud shoals created as the creek curled from one side of the canyon to the other.

Josie was suddenly filled with peace. Somehow, someway, she felt things would get better. Then she heard the sound of leaves rustling, like they were being stepped on. It wasn't the sound of the breeze or the birds. It came from the bushes directly behind her. She sat very still and listened again.

What could it be? For some reason she was sure it wasn't a person making the noise. She thought it had to be some kind of animal. Could it be a mountain lion? Was she safe? Was that peaceful, good feeling false?

No, Josie thought. *I've been through enough; God wouldn't do that to me today.* So she decided to investigate the source of the sound. She carefully got off the rock and worked her way through the thick willows to see what was making the noise.

As she slowly pushed aside the last of the willow branches, she couldn't believe her eyes. A young horse was standing twenty feet away, looking right at her.

Josie figured the foal was four or five months old. It already had proportions similar to an adult horse but it had a juvenile mane and tail which were about half grown.

Laying on the ground next to the foal was its mother, or at least what was left of its mother. Even from a distance Josie could tell the mare was dead. Thankfully, Josie remembered reading that a four or five month old foal would have been weaned from its mother's milk.

"Oh you poor thing," Josie whispered. "You're an orphan too!"

Two large ravens landed on the mare's body. The brown and white foal quickly spun around facing the birds, making a low moaning sound. It charged, slashing out with its forelegs.

The ravens flew up and landed in a tall ponderosa pine growing a few yards away.

"Caw, caw!" they said, taunting the foal.

Looking carefully at the young pinto, Josie realized it was a filly.

"You sweet thing," she said. "You're trying to protect your mother. You don't understand that she's dead."

The Lost Filly

Tears started streaming down Josie's face. She understood the pain and confusion the filly was feeling, because that was how Josie felt when she thought about her mom.

Josie wondered what she could do to help the pretty painted foal feel better. She also wondered who the horse belonged to.

Slowly, Josie eased out of the willows toward the filly. The young horse looked at her but didn't run away.

Josie stepped closer. Now the filly backed up, putting the body of its mother between Josie and itself.

Patience, thought Josie. *I don't want to scare it, but I'd sure like to be able to pet it.*

Very slowly Josie moved forward. The filly took one step back for each of Josie's two steps forward. She was gaining ground.

Josie and the filly engaged in this slow dance around the mare's body for what seemed like hours. Finally, Josie decided this was probably enough for a while.

The summer days in Oregon were very long. It didn't get dark in mid-June until nearly ten o'clock at night. She'd have time to come back down after dinner.

Josie would find some kind of treat to bring on her next visit. There had to be an apple or carrot in the house. Maybe that would do the trick.

Meanwhile, she'd try to ask some questions about who owned the land and any horses in the canyon.

4

Little Star

Aunt Sue was awake by the time Josie returned to the house.

"Where've you been?" asked Aunt Sue.

"I found the canyon trail and went down to the creek," said Josie. She wasn't going to say anything about the dead horse or the filly. Not now, at least, not until she had a better feeling about the future and how Aunt Sue would react.

"That's good," said her aunt. "Not many people use that trail anymore and now that the canyon is owned by the land trust, there aren't many people who hike along the creek either. So it's a great place for some solitude."

"What's the land trust?" asked Josie, delighted to get this kind of an opening to learn about the land ownership.

"Oh, they're some kind of environmental land preservation group. They buy land that they think is important to preserve. Then they manage it. Part of their style of management is keeping people and domestic animals, large and small, off the land. They don't even want you to walk your dog down there."

"So you mean the horse trails that Jack used to ride on aren't used anymore?"

"Nope. Once in a while the land trust's guides will lead a walk down there, showing people and the press all the good things they are doing. They are always looking for donations, so the guided walks help them raise money. Other than that, the canyon's goin' back to nature, so to speak.

"A few of us who live on the rim walk down there once in a while. But most of us are getting older and it's a long climb back up. So, there's not much goin' on down there."

That answered the first question, for the moment. The filly and dead mare didn't belong to the land trust. So now Josie would have to find out if someone in the area had lost a mare with foal.

Josie thought that would be a much trickier question to ask. Aunt Sue would wonder what made her ask it. Josie decided she'd just hold her questions for another time. First she'd have to see if she could get the filly to let her pet it.

"OK, Josie," said Aunt Sue. "I've been thinking about living arrangements for the time being. Jack's room should work well for you. The next-door bathroom will be yours. You'll be responsible for keeping it clean.

"We've got to get you more clothes. Out here in the summer, you'll need more jeans and shorts and shirts than you have.

"Things get real dirty from our powdery dust. We'd better get you another pair of sneakers, too. We'll go to town today and stop at Bi-Mart. They'll have everything you'll need for now.

"Can you cook?" continued Aunt Sue.

"I can fix soup and toast for dinner," said Josie. "And I know how to boil hot dogs. I'm good at warming up things in the microwave. Mom always said I was wonderfully self-sufficient."

"Those are all great things if you're in a pinch for food. But Sam and I try to eat things that are good for us. That means cooking from scratch. Things like making our own salad dressing with real olive oil and good vinegar and spices. We always eat a salad. Do you eat a salad with dinner?"

"No," answered Josie in a small voice. She never had a salad at dinner. Mom did not keep that kind of stuff in the fridge because it cost a lot of money and usually spoiled before it was eaten.

"OK, kiddo," said Aunt Sue. "This will be a learning summer for you. We'll take that self-sufficiency your mom talked about and move it up a notch to include healthy self-sufficiency."

Josie paused and thought about her uncle,

Sam. She remembered the first day they met. He had said, "Please just call me Sam. As an American, you already have a big *Uncle Sam*." His easy smile and soft voice made him nice to be around. He was strong and athletic with blond hair and blue eyes. Sam was one of the few men she was comfortable with.

Aunt Sue continued the discussion of responsibilities and told Josie that she could use her laptop computer as long as she turned it off when she was done.

Sue worked at the Sisters public library, so she showed Josie how to request books to check out and read. Aunt Sue said she would bring the books home whenever the librarian had her requests ready.

To Josie, this was one of the most significant things they had talked about. Josie's mom had never taken her to the public library. She had been able to check out books from the school library, but it was small, with a very limited selection of books about horses, the only topic Josie liked reading about.

Josie saw the list of horse books come up as Aunt Sue showed her how to search for books that she could request. There must have been a hundred books about horses!

Josie realized she would be able to read lots of horse stories whenever she wasn't working with *Little Star*.

That was it! The name just popped into her head. The filly had a little star in the middle of its shiny brown forehead. So that's what she'd call her, Little Star.

5

Apples and Carrots

Josie and Aunt Sue returned home from
shopping with several bags of practical out-
door clothes. This was more new clothing
than Josie had ever owned.

She even got two new pairs of sneakers!
One pair was black and one pair was white.
Aunt Sue had said that the black pair was
best for running around the yard and going
down into the canyon. Being black, they
wouldn't get dirty so fast.

If it weren't for missing her mom so
much, Josie would have thought she'd gone
to Heaven.

But mom always said, "Watch out when

things are going too good. Because before you know it, everything will fall apart."

Well, thought Jose. *Everything has already fallen apart, so maybe a little heaven is okay after all!*

Dinner had been heavenly, too. Aunt Sue's "cooking from scratch" was amazing. She had a cupboard full of herbs and spices that she used in everything. They'd had a dinner of grilled fish and salad. The only fish Josie had ever eaten before was breaded fish-sticks, which she loved. But this grilled fish was something entirely different and *sooo* good.

Josie had watched Aunt Sue cook. She made it look so easy. Josie now added learning how to "cook from scratch" to her list of things she wanted to do.

After dinner, Josie walked down the canyon trail carrying a bucket she'd found in the barn. It was now filled with carrots, apples and a rope. As she walked she thought about the past twenty-four hours.

She'd been so hopeful about having an exciting summer in the city, finally having some freedom for the first time. She thought about how that had all turned to ashes with her mother's death.

Now she was staying with her aunt, a woman who was almost a stranger. But Aunt Sue was nice to her. She wasn't warm and loving like her mom, but she was nice and willing to share. Maybe time would let them become good friends. Mom had always said good friends made life better. Josie decided she wanted to be good friends with her aunt.

After crossing the creek in the same shallow place, Josie sat on the same big rock to put on her shoes.

She listened very carefully trying to hear Little Star's movements, the way she had heard her before.

Nothing. Josie didn't hear a sound other than the light breeze in the trees. Even the ravens were quiet.

Josie slowly pushed her way through the willows. As she peeked out, there was no Little Star! The mare's body was still back near the big ponderosa pine. Ravens and buzzards were sitting on it, half asleep. But Little Star wasn't anywhere to be seen.

Tears started to well up in Josie's eyes. Mom was right! If things were going too good, just wait a few minutes and they would fall apart.

Suddenly Josie understood how much the filly meant to her. Without recognizing it before, deep down Josie had believed she'd be able to keep the filly. She'd thought she would be able to have a real horse. And what a special horse Little Star would have been, an orphan, just like her.

All the new clothes, the room with her own bathroom, access to the library and all the wonderful horse books were nothing compared to Little Star.

Josie collapsed on the ground in tears. The bucket fell out of her hand spilling the fresh apples and carrots onto the sand.

Josie cried and cried. She cried about her mother's death. She cried about how hard life could be. She cried about the dead mare and how terrible it was for Little Star to be alone…and she cried about the little filly that would never be hers.

Suddenly Josie's head popped up, eyes glazed with tears. What if Little Star wasn't just alone anymore? What if Little Star was dead? What if whatever had killed her mother had come back this afternoon and killed Little Star?

More tears rolled down Josie's reddened cheeks. Falling back on the ground, she pulled herself into a ball. Her sobs echoed off the canyon walls. She cried and cried, until there were no tears left.

Slowly, Josie uncurled herself. She'd better pick up the apples and carrots and head up the hill. Shadows were filling the canyon and it was starting to cool down. Soon Aunt Sue might start looking for her.

As Josie blindly reached out for the carrots, something touched her hand. It felt like hot breath. She let out a small scream and jerked back her hand, raising her eyes as she did so.

"Oh, no!" cried Josie. It was Little Star. She'd been reaching for a carrot at the same time Josie's hand stretched out for it. Her scream had made Little Star jump back.

New tears began streaming down Josie's cheeks as she took the carrot and held it out for Little Star.

Slowly the filly moved forward and Josie's heart raced.

She had only selected small carrots because she knew Little Star's milk teeth couldn't chew anything larger. Aunt Sue's fresh organic carrots had long green tops, so Josie turned the one she was holding around and offered the green top to the filly.

Very slowly Little Star moved forward. She stretched her neck, not wanting to get any closer than necessary. One more step and she'd be able to reach the carrot.

"Oh," breathed Josie, as Little Star's upper lip began to wiggle and stretch, reaching for the green leaves.

Using her nimble, fingerlike lips, Little Star flipped the greens around in a circle. Finally her short teeth caught some of the leaves and she jerked the whole carrot out of Josie's hand.

Backing up, Little Star shook the greens and slowly moved the wad into her mouth.

Her head bobbed up and down as she worked the carrot with her teeth.

Josie started to laugh. She couldn't help herself. Little Star looked so funny bobbing her head...and she couldn't believe she was laughing.

Little Star stopped chewing and just stood there looking at Josie as she laughed.

Josie stopped laughing and Little Star started chewing again.

Once the first carrot was eaten, Little Star

wanted more.

"Oh," said Josie. "So you like it?" And she offered the next carrot.

There were only six more carrots. Josie wanted this evening to last forever so she let Little Star beg and move closer before offering another carrot.

When the carrots were gone, Josie bit off a piece of apple and placed it on the open palm of her hand.

The soft, fuzzy muzzle slowly worked across her fingertips. The filly's nimble upper lip extended as it tickled the piece of apple across Josie's hand and into Little Star's mouth.

Again, Little Star bobbed her head up and down as she chewed the piece of apple.

Again, Josie couldn't help herself, she laughed. But this time Little Star kept chewing.

"I see," said Josie. "Bobbing your head up and down is your way of telling me you like the new flavor."

Little Star stepped forward again, moving closer than ever, looking for more treats.

"You're the sweetest friend I've ever shared an apple with," said Josie as she offered another piece.

Finally all the apples were gone and it was getting dark.

"I'd better go," said Josie, turning to leave.

At the top of the trail, Josie paused for one last look down the canyon. She could not see a thing.

"Good night sweet Little Star," she breathed. "I'll see you in the morning."

Slipping into the house, she heard Aunt Sue and Sam watching TV in the living room. She popped her head in and said good night, turning and running up the stairs to her room.

She was tired from the long day, but could she sleep?

6

The Challenge

Josie lay in her bed for a while, thinking about the incredible evening. She wished her mom could see Little Star. She loved that filly. She loved her brave spirit and her soft muzzle. And Josie loved her pinto color. She thought Little Star looked like a wild mustang.

That was it! Maybe Little Star was a wild horse. Maybe she didn't belong to anyone.

That hopeful thought and a prayer for Little Star's safety let Josie fall asleep.

During the night, Josie dreamed again about the Black Stallion's desert island. This time, like Alec in the movie, Josie was able to pet and run with the horse. But the horse in her dream wasn't a black stallion; the horse in her dream was a fiery pinto with a small star right in the center of its brown forehead.

The horse in Josie's dream was a lightning fast version of Little Star.

Morning arrived and Josie watched the sun do its pink and golden dance on the Cascade Mountains to the west of the house.

Even though it was a Sunday morning, both Aunt Sue and Sam were getting ready for work.

The library was closed on Friday and Saturday, but open on Sunday, so her aunt had to work.

Sam worked for the Sisters fire department, which meant his days on and off varied.

"You know where the food is," said Aunt Sue. "There's bread and peanut butter for a quick lunch if you want."

"Thanks. I'll be fine," said Josie.

"I know you will," said Aunt Sue. "I'll be home by two. I'll bring home the books you requested. Meanwhile, you can use my computer, watch TV or enjoy a walk in the canyon, if you want.

"Here's Jack's old cell phone. I charged it last night and it's still an active number. So if you have any problems or questions, just hit 'Mom' and you'll reach my cell phone."

As the vehicles pulled out of the driveway, Josie watched them leave. When they were out of sight, she gathered more carrots and apples, put them in her bucket with the rope and headed for the canyon.

After crossing the creek, she sat on the big rock and listened for Little Star's sound.

Nothing. No horse sounds at all. Just like the night before. But rather than cry, this time Josie pulled herself together and pushed her way through the willows to the place where she'd seen Little Star the day before.

Josie froze in horror. The mare's body had been ripped apart and dragged around. Hair and hide were spread over a large area. Rib bones curled toward the sky.

It was awful. Ravens and buzzards were so busy ripping, tearing and eating the carcass that they didn't even notice Josie's arrival.

Where was Little Star? Josie tried to be brave, remembering yesterday. But this was different. Yesterday Little Star's mother looked like a horse. Today, she looked like something out of a horror movie.

Could the creature that did this to the mare's body have killed Little Star too?

"Don't cry!" Josie told herself. But it was no use. Tears started to flow.

"Little Star, Little Star," Josie softly said. "Please come to me Little Star. I have more treats for you."

Nothing. Josie didn't hear any sound except for the gross chopping and flopping of the ravens and buzzards.

Then Josie felt the bucket push against her side. She slowly turned around and there was Little Star, trying to pull the green top of a carrot out of the bucket.

Relief filled Josie with joy. Her heart also filled with a conviction: Little Star was moving to the corral tonight, one way or another. Josie wasn't going to spend another night worried about the filly being eaten by a mountain lion or a pack of coyotes.

This meant that Josie had to teach Little Star how to walk with a lead rope. She'd read about teaching horses but she had never done it. Her love and a sense of urgency convinced Josie that she'd be able to lead Little Star up that steep canyon trail by the end of the day.

Josie began the lessons by getting Little Star familiar with the rope. She took the rope out of the bucket and laid it across the palm of her hand, placing a piece of apple on the far side of the rope from the filly. Little Star had to reach over the rope to get the apple.

Little Star's upper lip touched the rope. Suddenly her nostrils flared and warm, moist air surged out her nose in a loud puff.

Her eyes sparkled and her upper lip twitched. Little Star wanted the apple, in spite of having to deal with the strange rope. Slowly, her agile upper lip slid over the rope and she scooped up the apple segment.

The filly backed up to chew it.

Josie placed another segment on her palm in the same place. This time Little Star went right for it.

The lessons progressed. Eventually Little Star let Josie pet her. All the while Josie had the rope hanging across her shoulders or over her arms so that it often touched Little Star's body or legs.

Josie paused between treats, making Little Star come begging. She also gathered green grass, holding it out as a treat for Little Star.

After a while, as the sun warmed the canyon floor and a breeze blew the quaking aspen leaves, Josie lay down in a cool place and waited to see if Little Star would come to her. She did. Little Star actually lay down with Josie and fell asleep.

After their nap the training lessons began again. Josie had hooked the rope around Little Star's neck while she was asleep. When Little Star got up, the rope went with her.

Feeling the snaking rope around her neck, the filly reared up and struck out with her front legs. Then she took off and ran.

The rope flopped around Little Star's neck and dragged on the ground.

Josie was scared she'd tried to do too much, too fast. She was terrified that the filly might hurt herself running with the rope.

"What did I do?" Josie cried. "What could I do? Little Star can't spend another night down here."

"Patience," she said to herself. "Hold out a piece of apple, just as you've done before and let the filly come to you."

It worked. After running downstream and upstream for a few minutes, Little Star learned how to hold her head in a way that made the rope drag to one side, allowing her to walk without tripping on it.

The filly wanted the tempting apple more than she was afraid of the flopping rope, so she finally came back to Josie.

Josie didn't move as the filly reached for the piece of apple. Once it was eaten, Little Star raised her head and stretched out her upper lip, begging for more. Josie bit off another piece and offered it to the filly.

As Little Star began chewing the apple Josie started stroking her neck, touching the rope and making it rub against the filly's body.

Over time Josie was able to put a little weight on the rope without any reaction from the filly.

Finally, Josie tried to pull the lead rope. Little Star's reaction was to pull against it, not walk with it.

Josie thought she needed a halter if she was going to lead the filly up the trail. But all the halters she'd seen in the barn were too big.

Josie's confidence crumbled. She had to get the filly into the corral where she would be safe, but she didn't know how she was going to do it by the end of the day.

7

To the Corral

Josie was exhausted. She had spent the day trying to tame Little Star enough to lead her up the steep canyon trail and into the safety of the corral and barn. Heartsick, she was beginning to realize that there wasn't enough time in this day to train the young horse for the task.

The stress of the past two days and the tension of today's efforts were too much for Josie. Tears began flowing down her cheeks.

"All I do is cry," whispered Josie.

"You're doing great," came a male voice from behind her. Josie jumped to her feet. It was Sam.

"How long have you been there?"

"A few minutes," replied Sam. "I came home early from work and went looking for you, hoping we could have a chat. As I came down the canyon trail, I saw you with the filly. I watched you work with her and realized you were using goodies to make her come to you, so I've brought more apples and carrots," Sam said, as he held up a bucket.

"She likes you and she trusts you," Sam continued. "Where'd she come from?"

Josie pointed to the bones over in the shade of the tall ponderosa pine, about twenty yards away.

"I found her yesterday standing by her dead mother over there," said Josie.

Meanwhile Little Star watched Sam, but she didn't run. He held out a carrot, trying to get the filly to come to him.

Josie watched in amazement as the filly gingerly walked over to take the carrot out of his hand.

Sam reached into the bucket and pulled out another carrot. Little Star moved closer to him and grabbed the welcomed treat.

"I can't believe she's doing that. She's so calm with you," said Josie.

"I love horses, and for some reason they really like me," said Sam. "I've never had a horse not respond well to me."

"Wow! You're really lucky!" said Josie with wonder in her voice.

"Let's go take a look at the dead mare," said Sam.

Little Star fell in behind the two people as they strode over to the bones.

"At least this wasn't a mountain lion kill," said Sam.

"How do you know that?" asked Josie.

"Because a lion would have stashed any remaining carcass in bushes to keep it for its next meal. The buzzards and ravens wouldn't have scattered the bones like this so soon after a lion kill. And I can't imagine the filly living through a lion attack, anyway," replied Sam.

"What do you think killed her?" asked Josie.

"It's hard to say, looking at what is left now. But there are many things that can kill a horse. We lost Jack's horse to colic.

"It was a terrible thing," Sam continued. "Jack went to school and Sue and I went to work one morning. By the time we got home his horse was lying stretched out on the ground and wouldn't get up.

"We worked really hard to get him up while we waited for the vet. All in all, nothing worked. The horse died and Jack's heart was broken. That's why he joined the Marines right after high school graduation."

"That's terrible," said Josie. "I thought my heart was broken last evening when I came back down here and Little Star was gone. I can't even imagine how awful it would be to lose a horse I'd had for a really long time."

"Sue and I were broken up, too," said Sam. "Sue has a real hard time with losing something she loves.

"That's why she's kind of cool and distant with you right now. She loved your mom, even though they'd had problems over the years. She's really broken up over it right now and her way of dealing with grief is to withdraw."

"She's been nice to me," said Josie.

"I'm glad to hear it," said Sam.

"So, back to the filly and its mother," continued Sam. "I'd say the mare died of something other than a mountain lion attack. These scattered bones are the result of coyotes, ravens and buzzards feeding on the carcass.

"What's your plan for the filly?"

Sam's question startled Josie. She didn't expect him to ask her what she wanted to do.

"I was trying to train her to a lead rope so that I could lead her up the trail and into the corral tonight. I can't stand the thought of her getting killed out here," said Josie.

"That's a good plan," said Sam. "It's a wonder she has survived this long. Mountain lions work a large territory and the filly's probably been lucky that this area's lion is not hunting around here right now.

"OK. So I understand you want to lead the filly up the trail. That's not going to work. There isn't enough time to train her. She needs more time to learn how to walk with you leading her and she needs a small

halter, anyway. So we have to work out a
different plan.

"You noticed that she followed us over
here," continued Sam, looking back at Little Star, whose head was almost touching
Josie's back. "I think she is comfortable
enough to follow you up the trail. I'll walk
behind her to help her feel safe in the rear.

"Let's try walking around here like that
and I'll call Sue to see if she's home yet.
I'll ask her to open the corral gate and the
barn door. I'll have her park the vehicles
up at the front by the road to block the filly
if she bolts in that direction.

"I've never finished the front gate like I
should have, or we'd be able to close it off
from the highway," Sam said this shaking
his head in personal reproach.

"Anyway, if nothing scares her, we'll get
her in the corral and make her a happy little
girl."

Before she even realized what she was
doing, Josie ran over and hugged Sam with
all her might. Happy tears ran down her
cheeks.

"Careful there, sweetheart," said Sam,

smiling. "We have a long walk up that canyon trail and then we have to find out if someone has lost a mare with foal before you can call this filly yours."

"You mean if she doesn't belong to anyone else you'd let me keep her?" asked Josie.

"I'd be delighted to have you keep her. That empty corral has been a sore spot to me for a long time."

Josie and Sam worked with Little Star for about half an hour.

Using carrots and apple slices to lead her around, the filly quickly became an eager player of the new game. Little Star soon followed Josie like a devoted puppy dog and she didn't mind having Sam following her.

"Sue has everything ready for us," said Sam. "Let's see how this filly handles crossing the creek. Then we'll head her up the trail."

Little Star trotted across the water without hesitation.

"That's great," said Sam. "She's probably crossed a lot of water with her mom.

That will make her a great trail horse when she grows up. Crossing water is so often a big problem for many trail horses."

"Why?" asked Josie.

"I think it's because most corrals and pastures don't have streams to cross, so many young horses aren't comfortable with the noise and the sparkle of running water."

Satisfied that things were going well, Josie headed up the steep canyon trail.

The track was narrow and rough, but Little Star took to it like a mountain goat.

"Boy, Josie," said Sam. "You should see her from this end. This little filly has such confidence walking up this steep trail. I don't remember the last time I saw a horse do so well on such a rough trail – what a peach!"

They reached the top of the path and Little Star shied when she saw the house.

Josie stopped and held out a carrot. Little Star looked at the carrot, sniffed the air and seemed to decide everything was going to be alright. She took the carrot and began following Josie again.

Just as they reached the corral, a large, noisy truck barreled down the highway, a hundred yards from the corral gate. Little Star reared up and spun around, running toward Sam and the trail down the canyon.

Sam swiftly spread out his arms to block her way and soothingly said, "OK, baby girl, everything is OK."

Little Star stopped and snorted. Sam pulled out a carrot. The filly reached for it.

"That's a good girl," Sam cooed. "Let's go baby girl, let's get you into the barn and make you happy."

Aunt Sue had spread clean woodchips in the stall. Little Star walked into it with Josie as if she was just coming home from a long ride.

The filly smelled every corner. She soon discovered the hay manger with a small amount of Timothy hay. Next, she noticed the water bucket. Snorting into the water, she sprayed liquid all over her face. "You funny girl," laughed Josie.

Finally, Little Star found the grain bucket. Aunt Sue had put a few grains of malted oats in the bottom of the bucket. Little Star licked the oats, then banged the bucket against the wall as she searched for more.

"That will probably be your morning alarm from now on," said Sam.

Josie laughed again. "I hope so. I'd love to wake up every morning to that sound made by this little horse."

"Doc Peterson, the vet, is on his way," said Aunt Sue as she slowly approached the filly's new stall. "We haven't dealt with a foal in so many years that I didn't want to wait to call him. I wouldn't want to do anything wrong."

"That's great," said Sam. "Josie, we've got to be sure Little Star gets the right food right away. Remember what I said about colic? It's changing food that brings that on. We won't give her anything more until the vet gets here."

Josie began rubbing and scratching Little Star's neck. As she worked down the filly's neck onto the front chest area, Little Star stretched out her neck and her head went up. She started sticking out and wiggling her upper lip.

"She really likes that," said Aunt Sue,

with a big smile on her face.

Josie realized that was the first time she'd seen Aunt Sue smile since she'd arrived. She thought perhaps this filly was going to be good for everyone.

8

A Visit from the Vet

Doc Peterson looked at the filly from outside the stall. He was a tall, middle-aged man with kind eyes and gentle hands.

"She's a pretty little one," he said. "Let's see how she responds to me."

"She likes carrots," said Josie.

"Well, I'm glad to hear she's a real red-blooded American horse," said the vet.

Doc Peterson took the carrot Josie handed him and offered it to Little Star. She sniffed his hand and ate the carrot. He stroked her neck as she chewed it. She was fine with the handling.

"You said she was wild down there?" asked Doc. "She's doing awfully well now."

"That's because I've spent two days with her, teaching her to like people," said Josie.

"So you're going to be a horse woman, are you?" asked Doc.

"Yup!" responded Josie with a wide smile.

The vet stepped into the stall and Little Star soon became his friend, searching his hands for more treats.

The examination took quite a while. Doc Peterson checked her teeth and concluded she was about five months old. Her weight was a little light, to be expected he said, due to the conditions under which she had been living. Her agate colored hooves needed a farrier's file. The edges were chipped and the whole right, rear hoof needed proper shaping to help improve that leg's conformation.

After checking her neck for a microchip and not finding one, Doc decided that Little Star needed vaccinations for a number of diseases. He was a master at giving shots.

The filly never even knew she'd been given an injection.

As the vet was leaving, the discussion turned back to the question of who owned Little Star.

"OK," said Sam. "So you haven't heard of any missing mares with foals. I'll call the other vets in the area and check with them. I'll also put a notice in the *Nugget Newspaper* and see what happens. If we don't hear anything in the next week or so, I'll assume we have a new filly."

"That sounds good to me," said Doc. "I think she's a wild horse who wandered up the canyon. If the dam was run off by the lead mare in her herd, she and the filly could easily have followed the river and then the creek into this area.

"I don't see any need to contact the BLM. They don't want to deal with wild horses anyway. Keep me posted. I like this little girl and hope she's yours."

"Who's the BLM?" asked Josie as the vet drove away.

"They're a government organization who manages open range land. We have thousands of acres to the north and east of us that is open range land. They're the people you hear about who sell wild horses," said Sam.

Everyone had moved out of the barn as Doc Peterson left. Little Star was in her stall eating the goodies the vet had prescribed for her. Soon the filly started banging the empty grain bucket.

"I think your baby is calling," said Aunt Sue with a smile.

Josie ran back into the barn and slipped into the stall. Little Star started rubbing her neck against Josie's chest. Josie giggled.

Sam and Aunt Sue walked up to the stall's window and watched the girl and filly make a fuss over one another.

"They really love each other," said Aunt Sue, with a trace of sadness in her voice, as she thought about Jack and his horse.

"I think you're going to have to sleep in the barn with her tonight," said Sam.

"Oh! Could I?" asked Josie.

"I think you'll *have* to," said Sam. "She's going to need your company to keep from getting lonely and having a panic attack in the night."

"I'll get those goats we've talked about, tomorrow," said Aunt Sue. "We've, or at least I've wanted to get a few pigmy goats for a while. This is a great time to do it. They'll be company for Little Star and maybe I'll be able to get some fresh goat's milk in the deal."

It was getting late. Sue went in the house to make dinner. Sam stayed with Josie for a little while longer.

"I think she's a gift," said Sam. "Sometimes we get lucky in life to make up for all the hard times. I think this is one of the lucky times for all of us. Sue has wanted the goats, I've missed having a horse around and you need a best friend to love.

"Then, to top it all off, Little Star needs a safe place to grow up. It sounds like a winner to me."

Josie ran into the house when dinner was ready. She'd given Little Star more hay to keep her busy during dinner.

After dinner Josie packed up a few things, including the sleeping bag and old army cot Sam had given her, and headed

for a night of adventure sleeping with Little Star.

Settling down for the night in the stall on her cot with Little Star watching was like going to bed in Heaven.

"This is what a horse-crazy girl dreams about," she said to the filly.

Little Star lay down in the corner next to Josie. She'd had a big day, and like Josie, she was tired.

Josie was asleep before she knew it.

There were no storms or sinking ships in Josie's dreams. This night she joined Alec. He rode the Black Stallion and she ran alongside leading Little Star. Together they ran through cresting waves and receding surf with a bright sun tossing sparkling diamonds across the vast ocean. Little Star was as beautiful as the Black. Josie and the filly raced like the wind and kept up with the Black. Life was beautiful.

9

The Goats

Josie was awakened by a puff of warm air tickling its way into her ear. The sweet smell of Little Star filled the air.

"Oh! Hello there, you sweet thing," said Josie to the filly whose nose was now ruffling her hair. "That feels good. Do you want me to scratch your neck for you?"

Josie noticed dawn was just breaking. The barn was still dark but there was a little light outside.

"You wake up early, don't you?" said Josie. "Looks like we'll watch the sun rise together."

Standing up and wrapping her arms

around the filly's neck, Josie gave Little Star a big hug, then she began scratching the filly's chest.

Josie couldn't stop herself from giggling at Little Star's antics when she was being scratched in her favorite spots.

"You are so funny, stretching your neck and wiggling your lips," she said to Little Star.

"Let's get you something to eat so I can have some breakfast too."

Josie filled the manger with a large flake of Timothy hay, as the vet had recommended. Then she put the measured amount of grain and supplements into the bucket. Little Star quickly pushed Josie aside as she greedily reached for the grain bucket.

"OK, now you be good while I eat breakfast and wash off some of yesterday's dust."

Josie saw that Aunt Sue and Sam were already through with their breakfast. Sam stopped to talk to Josie as he headed out the door.

"Did you sleep well?" he asked with a smile.

"Better than I have in a long time," said Josie.

"Well, you and Little Star have a great day. I've already put the ad in the *Nugget* and I'll call the other vets this morning from work. If I hear anything important, I'll give you a call." With that, Sam slipped out the door, jogging to his pickup truck.

"I've left you some scrambled eggs, toast and fresh fruit," said Aunt Sue as she headed out the door after Sam. "Call me if you have any questions or problems. I should be home by about three and I hope to have the goats."

"Well," said Josie to herself in the now empty house. "I guess I won't be hanging out at the mall this summer."

****

After her shower, Josie ran out to the barn. Little Star was just finishing up her hay.

"OK, Little Star, we're going to let you out into the corral. You and I can spend the day exploring it and then do some other stuff together."

The filly loved getting out in the sun and having space to run. She and Josie ran around the corral, pacing side by side.

"It's a good thing I like to run," said Josie to the filly. "But you can sure outrun me!"

After the filly had explored every corner and run in many wide circles, the day warmed and the pair decided it would be nice to move back into the shaded barn.

Josie opened up the large sliding doors on both ends of the barn and the soft breeze filtered through the building, creating a cool oasis.

Josie spent the rest of the day teaching Little Star how to stand quietly while she brushed her.

The hair from Little Star's long winter coat came out in profusion as Josie brushed and curried her. The filly's brown spots looked light brown in her winter coat. Once the long winter hair was brushed out the pinto spots became a deep, rich chestnut color.

"I think you are going to be the most beautiful horse in the whole world," enthused Josie.

"Please, please, please, God, let me keep her," she prayed.

****

Three o'clock arrived before Josie realized it.

Aunt Sue parked her SUV's back end next to the corral gate. Then she walked around the barn and closed Little Star's stall door, locking the filly in.

"I'm letting the goats out into the corral," said Aunt Sue. "Once I have the gate closed again, I'll come and open up this door so that Little Star can meet her new corral mates."

"Did you hear that Little Star?" asked Josie. "You're going to have friends sharing your corral and keeping you company."

Aunt Sue quickly returned. "Let's see what everyone thinks of each other."

As the stall door slid open, it seemed like Little Star had understood every word Aunt Sue had said. She shot out of the stall with her short tail held high. Making a wide arc, she turned and looked at the goats. Her head went up and she gave a big snort. The goats bleated at her.

Slowly, Little Star made her way over to her new corral mates. She held her head low and breathed deeply, taking in their scent.

Aunt Sue had purchased three pygmy goats. They were this year's kids. Nearly full size, in spite of their young age, they were only about two feet tall. Good-natured, curious and gregarious, they wanted to meet Little Star.

Once Little Star and the goats met, noses actively touched and explored all parts of each other.

Then Little Star spun around and ran across the corral, tail in the air. When she stopped, she looked back at the goats as if to say, "Can't you run and play with me?"

Looking at the filly, the male Billy goat, bucked, kicked up his heels and ran after Little Star. This made the two female does run, and the game was on.

"Will she forget I'm her best friend?" asked Josie.

"I don't think so. Not as long as you feed her and don't neglect her," replied Aunt Sue.

"Sam hasn't called with any news, so I think that's really good news. I think you've got a horse," continued Aunt Sue.

"You're going to learn that horses are a big responsibility. But you'll love the work. It'll be good for you both.

"Speaking of work, we've got to set up some things for the goats," instructed Aunt Sue. "They need another water trough here in the corral. I bought a new one. It's on the back seat of the car. And we have to set up the other stall for them with woodchips and water.

"They'll eat hay and we'll spread it on the floor for now. We'll see how that works. Maybe we'll have to make 'em a new manger.

"I know before this is over," said Aunt Sue with a smile, "that Sam will say my goat's milk is costing him fifty dollars a gallon!"

The work was quickly finished and Aunt Sue headed for the house to start dinner.

Little Star and the goats busily checked out each other's stall. Then Little Star nibbled the goat's hay.

"I'll get you your own hay," said Josie and Little Star followed her into the filly's stall.

"So you do want to be with me," said Josie.

Little Star went over and licked her grain bucket.

"So maybe you only want me because I can feed you."

"Don't be too hard on her," said Sam as he walked into the barn.

"I didn't hear you drive in," said Josie.

"That's because you're worrying too much about losing Little Star's affection," Sam replied. "You found her. You began her training and you'll be her best friend forever as long as you keep the trust. Animals are honest creatures and they respect honesty. Let your love for her help you be honest with her in all your dealings, then don't worry about losing her love to the goats or anyone else, for that matter.

"The goats'll keep her company so that you can sleep in your own room and go to school. But she'll always be your horse.

"Speaking of which, none of the other

vets in the area have heard of a missing mare and foal. They all agree that if a mare was missing, they would know about it because mare's in foal need a vet.

"We're not going to lose her to another owner. I'm sure she's your horse. The real question is, will she let you sleep in your own bed tonight?"

Aunt Sue called out saying that dinner was ready.

"Let see how this goes," said Sam. "Will she start banging the grain bucket before long or will she and the goats be happy together for a while?"

****

All was quiet in the corral during dinner. Josie helped with cleanup and she even ran upstairs to take a quick shower.

The evening had cooled down and the air was sweet with the scent of summer flowers by the time Josie and Sam next visited Little Star.

"As I told you last night, she's got to sleep in a closed stall. So do the goats. We never know when coyotes, or cougars will visit the area and the filly and the goats are natural prey.

"So this will be the test," continued Sam. "Will the goats in the stall next door be enough company to keep the filly happy?

"If not, we may have to try putting one goat in the stall with her. If that doesn't work, we'll put them all together and they can have a slumber party!"

Josie and Sam spent some time playing with the goats to get them settled in their stall. Little Star watched everything.

After the goats seemed contented, Josie and Sam worked with Little Star. They scratched her tummy, rubbed her ears and scratched her chest. After all the attention, they gave her a little grain, turned out the light and walked out of the barn.

Sam stopped Josie as she headed toward the house. He put his finger to his lips indicating silence, then mouthed, "Follow me."

They quietly walked around the barn to a place where they could watch what the filly and goats were doing.

Little Star rattled her grain bucket. The goats bleated. Then she rattled the bucket again and the goats bleated again.

This went on for a few minutes. Finally, the goats all lay down together in one corner of their stall.

Little Star looked at the spot where the goats were lying down. She then walked over to the corner of her stall, getting as close to them as she could. She lowered her head, smelled the wood chips, scraping them with her foreleg, creating a small nest. Finally she bent her forelegs and lowered her body, lying down close to the stall wall. She tucked her muzzle into her side and closed her eyes.

Sam took Josie's hand, leading her away from the barn. Once they were far enough away, he sprinted to the house, holding his breath so he wouldn't burst out laughing.

They ran into the house, broke up in laughter and shared the whole experience with Aunt Sue.

"Aren't animals great?" said Aunt Sue.

"We can learn a lot about life from smart creatures like Little Star," said Sam. "She's been through a lot of recent trauma and yet look how willing she is to find contentment in her new home with her new friends."

"You're right," said Josie. "I hope that I can do as well.

"I never would have thought that I'd like goats," added Josie. "But these kids are just *too* cute."

"What do you want to name them?" asked Aunt Sue.

"You mean I can name them?" said Josie.

"Sure," said Aunt Sue. "You'll probably spend more time with them than me. Besides, I'll teach you how to milk 'em next spring, once they've had their first kids.

"They'll have to be milked early in the morning and you'll be up taking care of Little Star, so you'll be there anyway."

"Oh! That sounds like work!" Josie said with a smile. "I'll name them in the morning. I'm ready for bed right now."

****

"One more glorious day," said Josie to

herself as she curled up in her bed. "Mom, you'd love Little Star as much as I do and I think you'd like the goats."

She was asleep as soon as she closed her eyes.

She dreamed of sand, cool breezes and running beside her beautiful pinto. Life didn't get any better than that.

10

A New Friend

"Clang, clang, clang," rang the grain bucket in Little Star's stall.

Josie woke with a start. Then she heard the bucket again.

Jumping out of bed, she slipped on her jeans, shirt and shoes and raced down the stairs.

Aunt Sue was just serving up breakfast.

"I've got to take care of Little Star and the goats," Josie said as she ran out, banging the screen door.

"I think she's a wonderful kid," said Aunt Sue to Sam.

"You've got that right," said Sam. "Your sister may not have done everything the way you wanted her to, but she raised a great daughter."

In the barn, Josie noticed fresh hay had already been spread for the goats and laid in Little Star's manger. Little Star was still licking the grain bucket and batting it around with her nose.

"So you've already had breakfast!" said Josie. "I ran out here because I thought you needed help, but you're already taken care of and I haven't had my breakfast."

Smiling at her filly, Josie gave her a hug, brushed her for a minute, then returned to the house.

As she sat at the breakfast table she said, "Thanks for feeding the animals, and letting me sleep in."

"We don't want you to get as spoiled as that filly, but you've had a few long days and we thought you deserved the extra sleep," said Sam.

"What's your plan for today?" asked Aunt Sue.

"I thought I'd try and put the new halter on Little Star. If she does real well, I'll work at leading her around the corral."

"Sounds like a great plan," said Sam.

"What are you going to name the goats?" asked Aunt Sue.

"How about Jack for the buck and Jill and Joan for the two does?"

"That's cute. I like it. Just hope your cousin, Jack, doesn't mind," said Aunt Sue.

"Oh! I didn't think about that," said Josie.

"I'm just kidding. He'll love the names. I'll tell him in my next email that we have a new 'Jack' living with us. I'm sure he'll enjoy hearing about that."

****

Aunt Sue and Sam left for work. Josie quickly cleaned up the kitchen and went back out to clean the stalls and work with Little Star.

As Little Star rubbed her head against Josie's chest, Josie rubbed the new halter against the filly's neck and head. Little Star accepted the new tack item without a problem. Soon Josie had slipped it over the filly's face and fastened it.

Little Star shook her head and began

rubbing her head on Josie again. Josie scratched the filly's ears and slowly put a little pressure on the halter's rope ring.

Little Star raised her head but didn't seem to mind the new sensation.

"You're a good girl," said Josie as she opened the stall door to the corral.

Little Star ran out the door with her short tail waving in the air like an ostrich plum in a Musketeer's hat. She bucked and kicked for the first time.

"We don't want that to become a habit," said Josie, as she let the goats out into the corral.

Little Star ran toward the goats, then faded to the right at the last second.

"So you want to play?" said Josie.

The goats had decided the same thing and started running around in circles, bucking and kicking.

"Maybe this is rodeo day," said Josie, watching everyone having a great time.

Josie noticed a girl about her age was sitting on a bicycle out by the main road, watching the animal show.

Josie waved and then signaled for the girl to come join her.

Josie stepped to the fence as the girl peddled her bike over, "Hi, I'm Josie. What's your name?"

"I'm Tina," said the girl as her green eyes flashed a warm smile under her mass of strawberry blond hair. " Is this your horse?"

"We think so," said Josie. "We have to wait a few days to be sure.

"Do you like horses?" asked Josie.

"Oh, sure. We have four. One for each of us in the family. Do you ride?" asked Tina.

"No," said Josie. "But my uncle will teach me how to break Little Star and then I'll learn how to ride her."

"You could come over to my place and learn to ride our horses. I can show you the basics and then you'll be ready to ride when Little Star is old enough."

"You mean you'd share your horses with me?" Josie asked, incredulous that this pretty, warm girl would be so generous with a stranger.

"Oh, sure," said Tina. "My mom would not mind. There aren't a lot of kids our age in the area. She'd be happy I met a friend who likes horses."

"Awesome! That would be really cool," said Josie. "Would you like to come in the corral and help me teach Little Star how to walk nicely with a lead rope?"

"Sure. Then you can come over and see my horses."

"That's a great plan," said Josie as she opened the gate for Tina.

Tina knew a lot about horses, so she and Josie quickly became good friends. Josie told Tina about her mom dying and how she now lived with her Aunt Sue and Sam.

Then she shared Little Star's story.

"Wow, that's an awesome story. I sure hope the vet is right and that no one else can claim her," said Tina. "It would be a lot of fun to help you train her so that we could ride together with you on your own horse.

"Maybe you could ride with us in the Sisters Rodeo Parade."

"My cousin Jack used to ride in that

parade. I'd love to do that!" said Josie.

****

After a lot of time working with her, Josie and Tina finally got Little Star to calmly walk beside them with the lead rope.

"Little Star is a really smart horse," said Tina. "She learns really fast."

"I think she's extra smart because of all the problems she lived through. She had to be smart to keep from getting killed by wild animals after her mother died," said Josie.

"So, let's have lunch," added Josie. "My Aunt Sue is showing me new things to cook. I'll make us a nice avocado, tomato and lettuce sandwich. Doesn't that sound great?"

"I really like peanut butter and jelly," said Tina quietly, just a little embarrassed.

"OK. We'll have peanut butter and jelly. That's easier anyway!"

****

After lunch, Josie called Aunt Sue and asked if it was okay to go over to Tina's and ride her horses.

Aunt Sue already knew Mrs. Purdy, Tina's mother. She told Josie it was okay to ride the horses as long as Mrs. Purdy approved.

Before leaving, Josie made a final check to be sure that Little Star and the goats had water. She also made sure the corral gate and all doors were locked. Then she followed Tina to her house.

****

"I'll put saddles on my horse Ginger, and mom's horse Buddy, the bay. You can ride Buddy because he's really, really calm. That's why mom likes him," said Tina. "Then I'll show you how to sit in the saddle and the right way to hold the reins."

Buddy was about fifteen hands— medium height for a horse. Josie was somewhat small for her age, so it was a long way up to the stirrup and saddle.

"Mom uses a mounting block," said Tina, who was taller than Josie. "I guess that'll be a help for you too."

Once Buddy was standing next to the mounting block, Josie stepped up on it.

"Oh, this is much better," said Josie.

Tina showed Josie how to insert her foot in the stirrup, grab the saddle horn and reins with her left hand, grab the cantle with her right hand and pull herself up, swinging her right leg over the horse.

"Wow!" said Josie. "I didn't realize how hard it would be just to get up in the saddle."

"Just wait 'til we trot if you think getting on is hard," said Tina with a smile.

Tina adjusted the stirrups for Josie and then mounted Ginger, her buckskin, without the aid of the mounting block.

"Wow! You made that look easy," said Josie.

"Well, if you'd been riding since you were six years old, it would be easy for you too," said Tina. "Now let's walk the horses around the arena."

Josie was having the time of her life. She worried a little about leaving Little Star all alone and then remembered what Sam had said about the goats. They were company for the filly so that Josie didn't have to be with her all the time.

Josie thought that learning to ride was a good enough reason to leave Little Star alone. She really wanted to be able to ride Little Star as soon as the filly was old enough to break. By learning to ride now, she hoped that she'd be able to do all the filly's training, not just the ground work.

For just a split second her mom's words, "Watch out when things are going well. Because before you know it everything will fall apart," crept into Josie's mind. Things were going so well now, she really didn't want things to fall apart.

Josie had Little Star, the horse of her dreams. She also had a new friend who was teaching her how to ride. Josie hoped her mom could see her now. In spite of missing her mother and dealing with that terrible grief, in many ways her life was better than it had ever been.

11

The Stranger

By Friday Josie and Little Star had developed a regular daily schedule.

Josie woke up at about six in the morning, fed the filly and the goats, returned to the house for breakfast, cleaned the kitchen, returned to the corral and worked Little Star until lunch. Tina rode Ginger over after lunch and the girls worked together with Little Star.

Ginger's presence added a new dimension to the filly's training. Tina said it was important for the filly to accept other horses.

Little Star soon looked forward to Ginger's arrival, even offering a gentle nicker as the horse walked up to the corral.

After working on a few lead rope exercises with Little Star, the girls always rode double on Ginger to Tina's place for afternoon riding lessons.

****

An appointment with the farrier broke up Wednesday morning's activities. He filed Little Star's ragged hooves and adjusted her right back foot to straighten out the hock. He told Josie that this early effort would ensure Little Star's rear legs grew strong and straight, making her a powerful mount for many years.

The only change to Friday's schedule was the result of Aunt Sue having a day off from work.

After Friday's breakfast, Aunt Sue suggested that Josie might want to come home a little early from riding lessons. She said they could work together on a special dinner.

Josie wanted to learn more about Aunt Sue's cooking, so she readily agreed to return home by three o'clock.

As Josie approached the house at the agreed upon time, the early afternoon breeze cooled her face. She noticed an unfamiliar vehicle sitting near the front of the house. It was a large, sleek, dark blue Harley-Davidson motorcycle with deep saddle bags, stuffed to overflowing.

Josie wondered if Jack had come home with a friend.

She started to open the screen door at the front entry, when she heard a loud, angry voice.

Josie froze. She may have forgotten what her father looked like, but she would never forget what his awful, angry voice sounded like.

She had stopped mid-step. Lowering her foot, she listened.

"You ugly witch! You think you can keep her from me?" yelled Josie's father. "I'll teach you not to cross me!"

Josie knew what would follow. Her mother had been beaten by this man so many times Josie had lost count of the number of visits they had made to the emergency room.

It took her mother years to find the courage and means to escape the brutality.

Now the monster was threatening Aunt Sue.

Josie's first impulse was to run in and try to help. But she knew from experience that Pete would simply throw her aside and do whatever he wanted to Aunt Sue.

She had to think. She had a cellphone. She could call Sam.

Quickly, Josie pressed Sam's number. When he answered she told him what was happening.

"I'll be right home," said Sam. "Stay where you are and call 911. The sheriff may be able to get there before me.

"Sue's strong and smart; she'll be able to hold him off until we get there. But don't you get in the middle of it or you'll get hurt."

Josie called 911 and had to stay on the line for what seemed like forever giving the operator all the information he wanted.

Meanwhile the argument raged. Pete wanted Josie to come to California and live with him. Aunt Sue was having none of it.

Suddenly there was a loud crash. Josie ran into the house. Someone had to help Aunt Sue and Sam wasn't there yet.

"There you are, you little witch. You're coming with me," Pete said while his right hand held a fire poker high in the air.

Josie quickly assessed the situation. Aunt Sue was standing behind Sam's easy chair, keeping it between Pete and herself. But Pete was easing himself forward, his body language threatening Aunt Sue with the poker. The couch was between Josie and Pete, as he was standing in the center of the living room.

A small woman with muddy blond curls stood next to the fireplace, cowering.

Pete's dark lips curled up in a wicked smile, showing his crooked, yellow teeth.

"It's the spoiled little witch!" Pete snarled, looking at Josie, "Get any money there is in the house. You're coming with me."

"How can you take me? You're riding a motorcycle and you already have a passenger," Josie said, pointing to the woman.

"Don't worry about it. You'll fit. Now get the money and get back here so we can leave."

"She's not going anywhere," said Aunt Sue with a hard authority in her voice that Josie had never heard before.

Pete stepped toward Aunt Sue pulling the poker back, ready to smash a forceful blow on the unrelenting woman.

Josie screamed louder than she thought possible. Pete turned, lunged and swung at her, breaking a lamp as the poker crashed down at the end of the couch.

"Drop the weapon!" shouted the sheriff, entering the room with his gun drawn.

Pete didn't skip a beat. He raised the poker and sneered at the sheriff.

"She's my daughter and I'm taking her home. You can't stop me!"

"Try me," said the sheriff.

Sam ran into the room. "Sue! Are you OK?"

"Yes," she said. Then turning back to

Pete, she added, "This monster may be Josie's biological father, but he long ago abandoned her. He only wants her now because he thinks he can collect some kind of aid from the state because her mother is dead."

"She's my blood, not yours, you witch." Pete sneered. "You'll never be able to keep her from me."

"I've got news for you," said Aunt Sue. "I've already checked all this out. You owe thousands of dollars in back child support because my sister wouldn't go after you for it. She preferred to live in poverty, with no assistance from the government, just so no one in Children's Services would try to chase you down and get you to pay what you owed. She was afraid you'd come after her and she preferred being poor to being beaten or dead.

"I've got the proof I need to sic the government on you if you give us any trouble with adoption. You'll give your consent to Josie becoming our legal daughter or, by God, I'll see you go to jail for as long as you live."

"That all sounds good to me," said the

sheriff. "Meanwhile, I'm cuffing you for attempted assault with a deadly weapon. You're coming with me."

****

As the sheriff put Pete in his police cruiser, the woman who had been standing next to the fireplace slid out of the room, through the front screen door and mounted the motorcycle.

"Follow us, sugar. Then you can bail me out," called Pete to the woman.

"Sure," she said, but it didn't sound like she meant it.

Standing at the front screen door, watching the sheriff leave, Aunt Sue tightly hugged Josie and Sam. She was still shaking from anger and fear.

"I thought for a minute he was going to kill me," said Sue.

"Was that when I heard the crash?" asked Josie.

Aunt Sue nodded her head. "How did the sheriff get here?" she asked.

"Josie heard Pete's voice before entering the house. She called me and then called

911," said Sam.

"I owe you my life for thinking fast and making those calls," said Aunt Sue, looking at Josie. "You and I would never have been able to stop that man if he'd really come after us with that poker."

"When I was little I watched too many times what he did to my mom," said Josie. "Why is he like that?"

"Who knows," said Sam. "Some people are just put together with a screw loose."

After taking all this in, Josie asked,

"Are you really going to adopt me? Will I become Josie Kent? Will I really be able to live here with you forever?"

Aunt Sue now wrapped both her arms around Josie and gently ran one hand through her hair. Slowly rocking the girl, Aunt Sue said, "You're my new angel, sweetheart. I once had hoped to have a girl and now I've got one."

"I was so afraid when my father said I had to go with him," Josie said. "Mom always said that when things were going good watch out because before you know it everything will fall apart.

"Things have been so wonderful these past few days that I've been waiting for the bad news. I knew something would make it all fall apart."

"OK, sweetheart," said Aunt Sue. "Your mother was a good, brave woman but she led a hard life and that's why she believed that. She's now at peace and you know she is watching over you."

"Yes," said Josie, "I believe that. It's the only reason I can go on."

"Now you've moved to a better place, too, so let's give you a new thought to live by," said Aunt Sue.

"My mother, who was also your mom's mother, always said, 'Into every life a little rain must fall, and then the sun will shine again.'

"Do you see the difference? We will always have difficult days, but we are a family who loves each other. We're strong and committed to one another. The sun will always come out, after the rain."

****

That night, in Josie's dream, she saw herself riding on a beautiful chestnut colored pinto mare with a little star on its forehead. She was riding next to Alec and the Black Stallion.

They weren't on the desert island this time. They were in a lush, green meadow, surrounded by tall ponderosa pines. The jagged snowcapped peaks of Oregon's Cascade Mountains wrapped behind the forest like a sleeping dragon standing guard. Clear blue skies crowned the picture.

"Josie," said Alec, "You're home. The sun is shining."

Slowly awakening from the dream Josie smiled in her growing sense of peace that her mom was watching over her and would always be close. She also felt secure in the comfortable love of her new family. Finally, Josie knew that regardless of what challenges the future held, she, her family and Little Star would face them together.

The end ... for now!

Acknowledgements

Writing a book without help from "readers" would be impossible for me. Writing is known as a lonely business. I love teamwork and writing with reader input makes the process feel like a team effort.

Thank you to all the readers who have helped me with this book and special thanks to two very exceptional readers, Barb Dickson and Justin Collins, who have added many great ideas. Thanks, also, to Cheryl Fugate, Merle Henn, Cile Tice, Emily Boraas, Marty Sordorff, Jeri Buckmann, and Sandy Mayernick.

Many thanks to my wonderful, long-suffering husband, Claude. He has been reading and re-reading my books ever since my first, written in 1984. He has always had good ideas for improving what I've been working on and thankfully, he catches most of my spelling errors and many typos.

Finally, thanks to my son, Rob Russell, who is a much better writer and artist than I. Rob's tips and ideas have been priceless.

I hope you'll all be with me for the next book in this series.

Jean Russell Nave
ww.horsecrazybooks@yahoo.com

Jean, on her horse when they were both five years old.

About the Author

When author Jean Russell Nave was Josie's age, she had a secret. For many years Jean had great difficulty reading and spelling.

When she was young, schools did not offer special education teachers. Most schools didn't even recognize special learning needs.

Jean fought long, hard mental battles as she tried to learn to read and spell as well like classmates. She eventually developed methods to master these two demons well enough to achieve good grades, graduating high school as class valedictorian.

At twenty-eight years of age Jean learned that there was a name for the learning challenge she faced: *dyslexia*. Finding out that she was not "dumb" was a big relief and it was comforting to learn she wasn't alone with the problem.

Jean's best friend during those challenging school years was her buckskin quarter horse mare, Ginger. When life got too rough, Jean would go for a ride and cry on Ginger's shoulder.

It is these wonderful days, months and years with Ginger that Jean uses as the primary inspiration for her horse stories.

Having retired from an exciting professional career which included working in local television, national public speaking and writing self-help books, Jean now is able to do something really special: spend time feeling like a young, horse-crazy girl, and writing about her adventures.

Sponsoring
Freedom Hills Therapeutic Riding Program

Jean has been using the profits from her books to help non-profit organizations since 2002, when she wrote *Wildfire Hits Black Butte Ranch*. All profits from that book went to fire rescue and the local historical society.

Her next endeavor was a series of children's books about the rescued Scottish Terriers she and her husband adopted, *The Harry and Lola Adventure Series*. All profits from those books go to Aberdeen Scottish Terrier Rescue of Oregon and Southwest Washington.

It was only natural for Jean to want royalties from this book, *The Lost Filly*, to support a horse-related program. Thanks to her friend and supporter, Barb Dickson, Jean learned about Freedom Hills TRP.

Since 1982, Freedom Hills Therapeutic Riding Program, a non-profit 501(c)3 organization, has been bringing horses and people with disabilities together.

They are dedicated to improving the quality of life for the disabled and challenged by bringing people and horses together.

Freedom Hills TRP offer equine facilitated therapy to individuals with physical and/or emotional challenges, as well as kids at risk and military veterans, with their physician's approval. Classes are conducted by trained instructors and assisted by volunteers and physical therapists when needed. As always, safety is their highest priority.

To learn more or make a donation, please visit their website: www.freedomhills.org

PORT DEPOSIT MARYLAND

Other books by this author:

The following series of illustrated children's books support Scottie rescue.

Harry and Lola Meet Starprancer introduces readers to a winged angel horse who helps wild horses.

www.amazon.com/dp/1490546073

Harry and Lola Meet the Dragon brings readers face to face with a dragon who first wants to eat Lola but later wants to be a good dragon.

www.amazon.com/dp/1478286903

Harry and Lola Meet MacDuffer is a fun adventure about learning how to play golf. The magical spirit of golf, MacDuffer, helps the Scotties master the game.

www.amazon.com/dp/1482078279

**Two collection books give the reader
three stories in each volume:**

The Harry and Lola Christmas Collection's three stories inspire, delight and enlighten readers to the joys of the Christmas season.

www.amazon.com/dp/1475060831

The Harry and Lola Collection introduces readers to rescued Scotties, Harry and Lola and the world they live in, including a raccoon family, eagles, swans and other animals.

www.amazon.com/dp/1475060831

*Please remember, all profits from the sales
of these books go to help Scottie rescue.*

Learn more at www.harryandlola.org

34233382R00066

Made in the USA
Charleston, SC
01 October 2014